For Mags, for your love and encouragement
JH

The Big

Brown Lazy
Dog

To Grace & Molly,
Happy Reading,
John Halvorsen

This is the story
about a dog, who was
BIG.
He was also brown,
which doesn't matter,
because he could have been any

colour.

But it is about the day he fell asleep
and what happened when no-one could
wake him up.

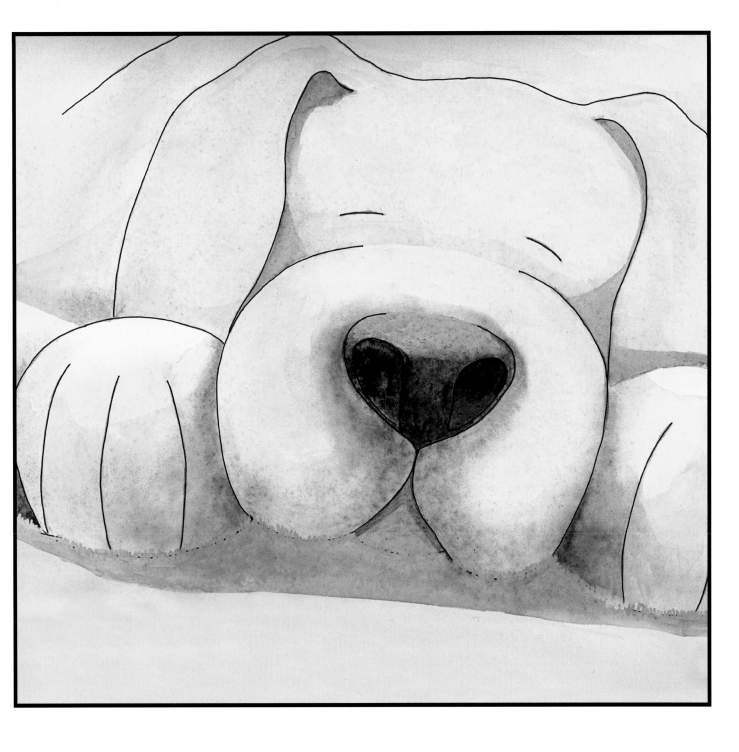

It was a warm summers day and
Big Brown Dog lay sleeping in the
sunshine.

As he slept, Charlie Chuckles, The Rooster
approached.
"Good morning Big Brown Dog,
would you mind moving out the
way.

You see, the Quick Red Fox is after my rather
gorgeous feathers.
Do be a nice chap and move so that I can pass."

But Big Brown Dog just lay snoozing and
didn't budge an inch.
SO..........

Charlie Chuckles the Rooster,
had to climb over.
Very silly he looked too.

"Big Brown Dog you must be the
laziest dog in the whole wide world," he
said and stomped off, very annoyed indeed.

Before long, Dot and Flo,
the two Grumpy Sheep came by.

"Excuse us," said the sheep, "but could
you please move. We're on our way to
avoid the Quick Red Fox. He intends
stealing our beautiful fluffy wool."

But Big Brown Dog took no notice, he
didn't even bat an eyelid. He just kept on
sleeping.

SO...........

Dot and Flo, the two Grumpy Sheep
had to climb over.
Oh Calamity! What a long way down.

"Big Brown Dog, you must be the laziest
dog in the whole wide world," they said
and left very annoyed indeed.

As the day wore on, Pigwig Small approached. "Ahem!" he said, clearing his throat.

"Excuse me, Big Brown Dog, but would you mind letting me past. The Quick Red Fox is after my beautiful hair so if you would just move I can squeeze past."

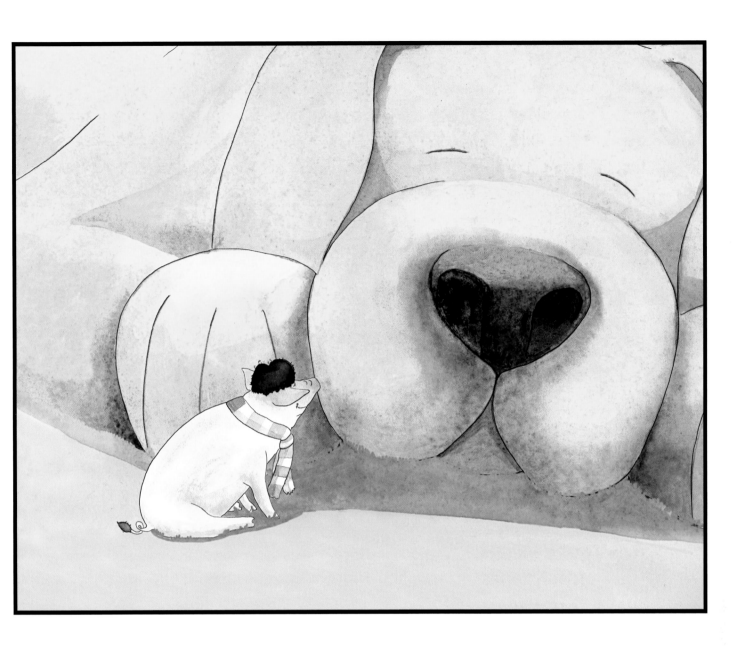

But.... Big Brown Dog just lay there, fast asleep, not moving one bit.

Pigwig Small, just couldn't believe it,

SO.........

He had to climb over......
Oh my goodness, not an easy task for a
Small Pink Pig.

"Big Brown Dog, you must be the laziest
dog in the whole wide world," he said and
trotted off most displeased.

He did!

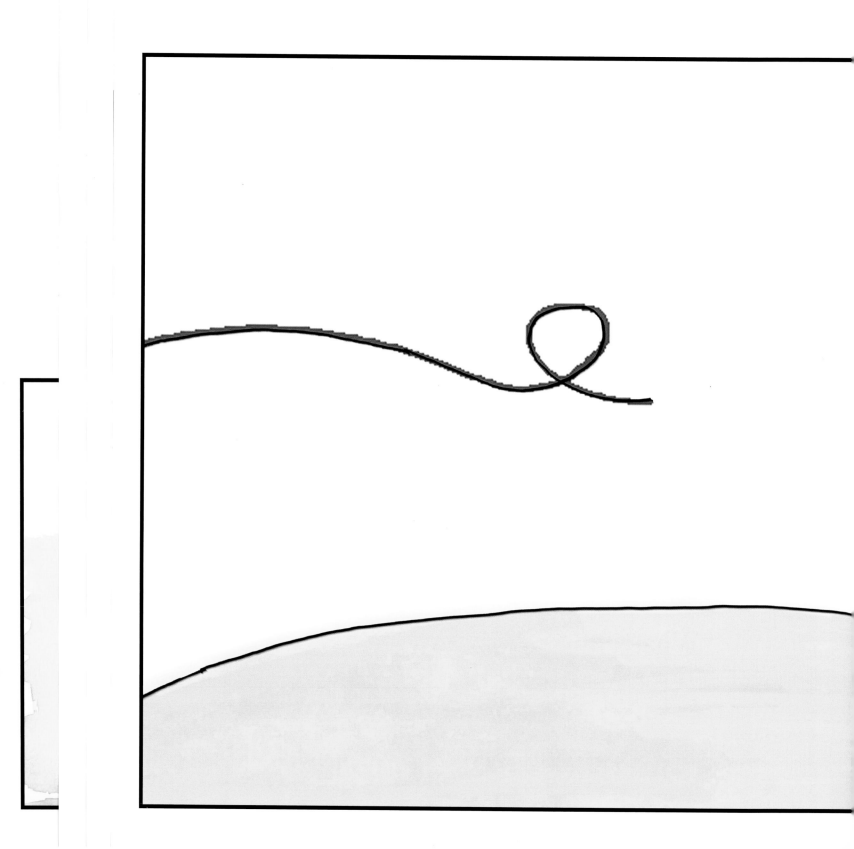

The Quick Red Fox
jumped over the sleeping
Big Brown Dog.

Straight into a trap.
"Got him," the animals cheer. "And all
without that Big Brown Lazy Dog," they
said laughing.

"Hello chaps," said The White Duck.
As she walked straight past her friends,
right up to the Big Brown Dog.
"He won't let you past, you'll have to
climb," they shouted.

"Who me? Never," she said.

SO.......

Leaning forward, she pulled two large earplugs from under the Big Brown Dog's ears.

Suddenly, his two eyes snapped open.

To everyones amazement, the Big Brown Dog lifted his head, yawned, stretched, then walked off, leaving a clutch of six warm eggs he had been guarding for The White Duck, while she took a bath.

SO.......

He hadn't really been asleep, only resting his eyes while he listened to some music. Everyone felt awful, they said sorry to the Big Brown Dog. All except for the Quick Red Fox that is. He found it hilarious.

SO.......

Don't judge others,
you might end up
feeling silly.
Sometimes it's better
to let sleeping dogs lie,
especially

Big Brown
ones!